This book belongs to:

_____

_____

_____

Incy Wincy Spider

Keith Chapman

Jack Tickle

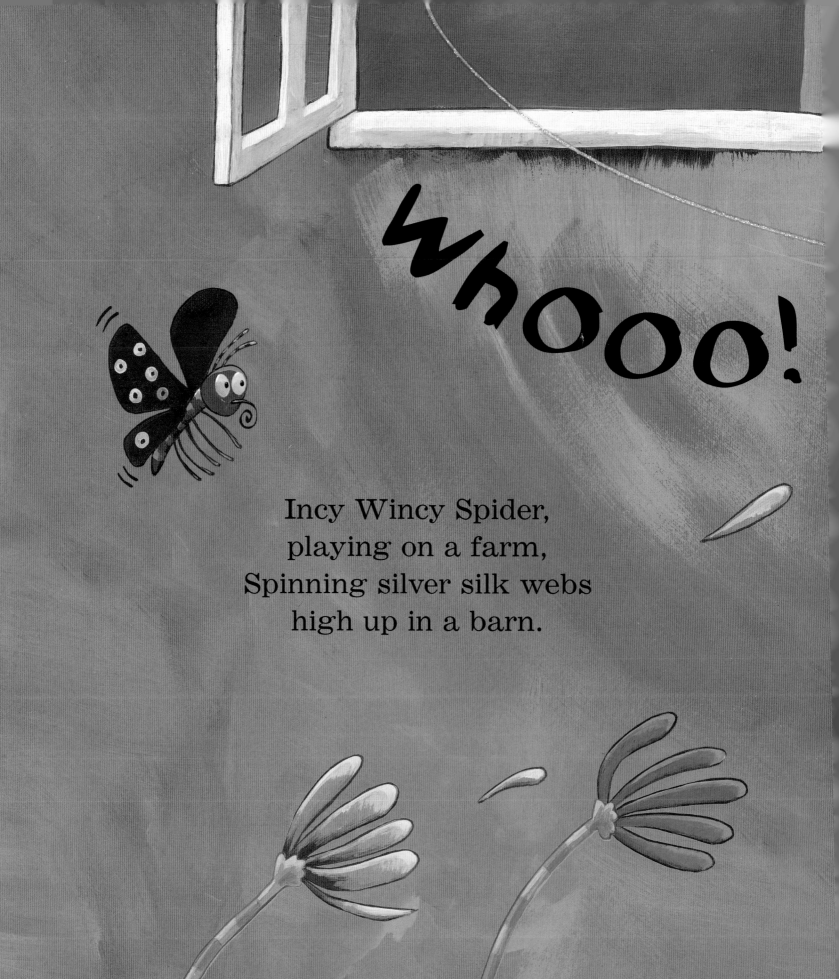

Whooo!

Incy Wincy Spider,
playing on a farm,
Spinning silver silk webs
high up in a barn.

From an open window
a gust of wind blows WHOOO!

whooooosh

And Incy Wincy Spider
with a WHOOOOOSH goes too!

Incy Wincy Spider
is flying, there he goes!
He drifts onto a pink pig
and dangles from its nose.

OINKKK! grunts the pig
with Incy climbing up his snout.
And Incy Wincy Spider
is catapulted out!

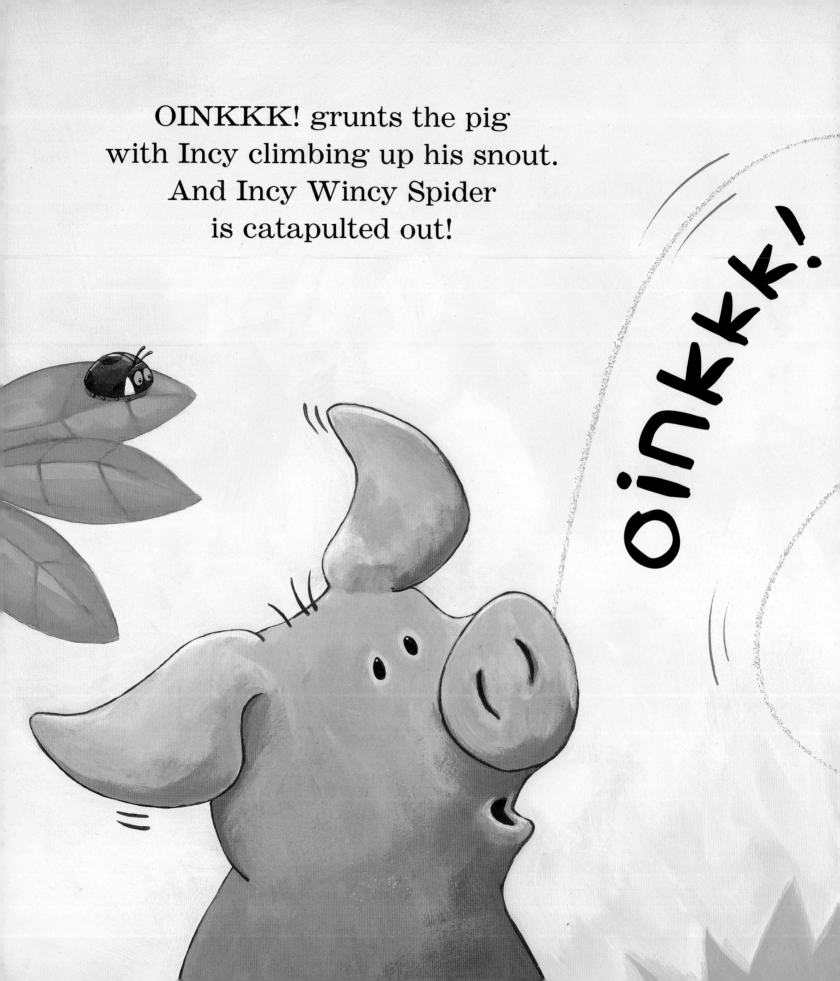

Incy Wincy Spider,
he doesn't think it funny.
He's tangled on a gray goat
and calls out for his mommy.

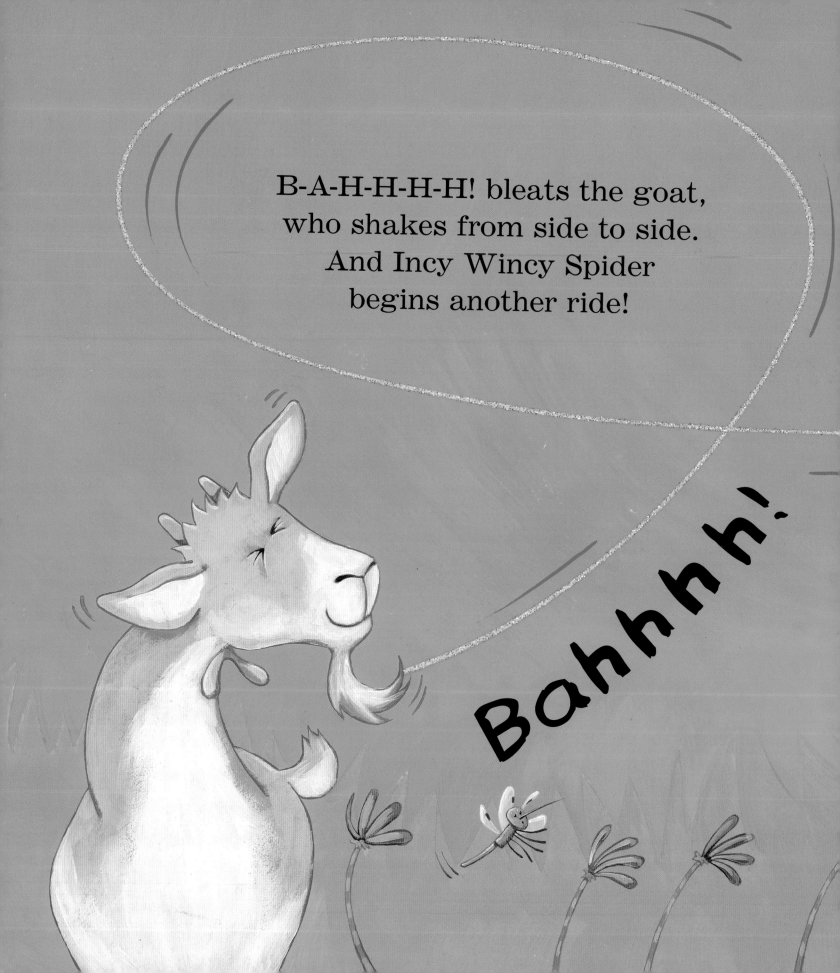

B-A-H-H-H-H! bleats the goat,
who shakes from side to side.
And Incy Wincy Spider
begins another ride!

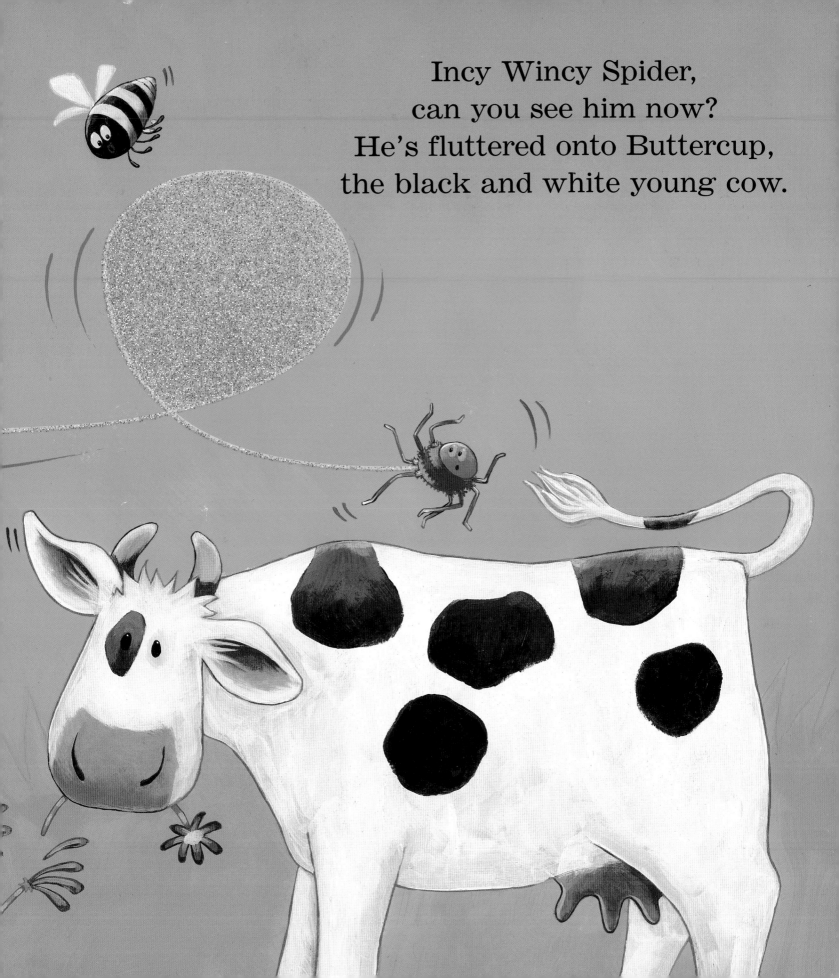

Incy Wincy Spider,
can you see him now?
He's fluttered onto Buttercup,
the black and white young cow.

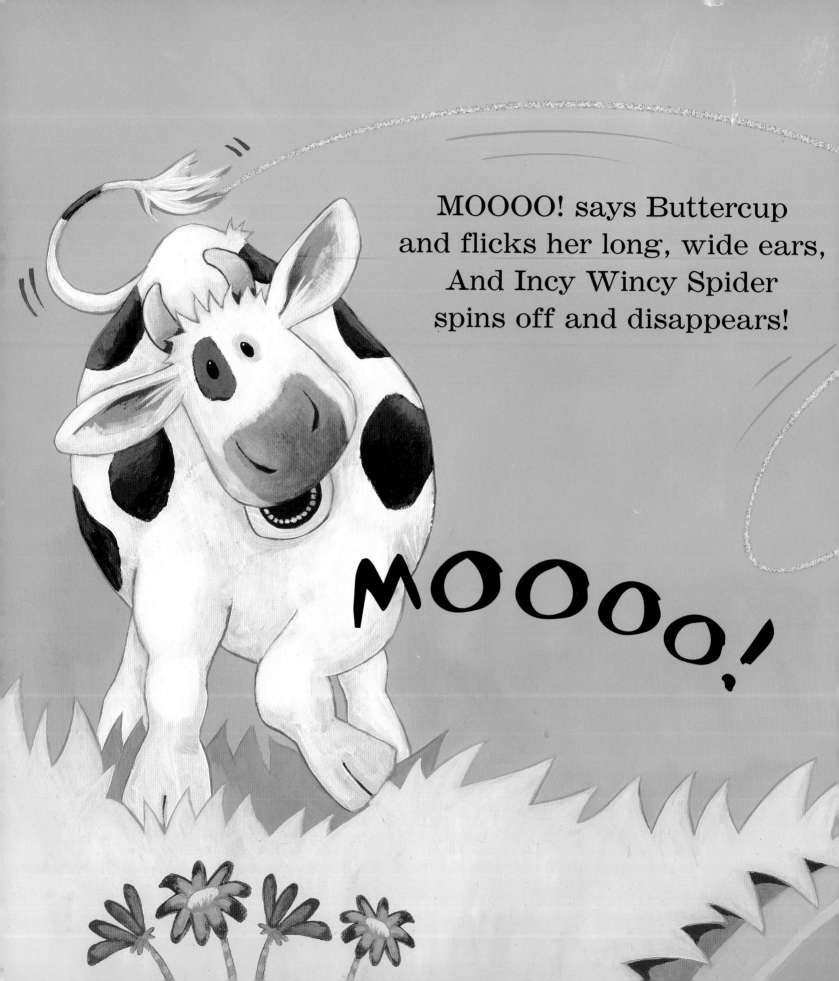

MOOOO! says Buttercup
and flicks her long, wide ears,
And Incy Wincy Spider
spins off and disappears!

MOOOO!

Incy Wincy Spider,
gliding through the air.
He hangs onto a duck's beak
and tickles under there.

QUACK! honks the yellow duck
and gives a great big sneeze.
And Incy Wincy Spider
floats off in the breeze!

QUACK!

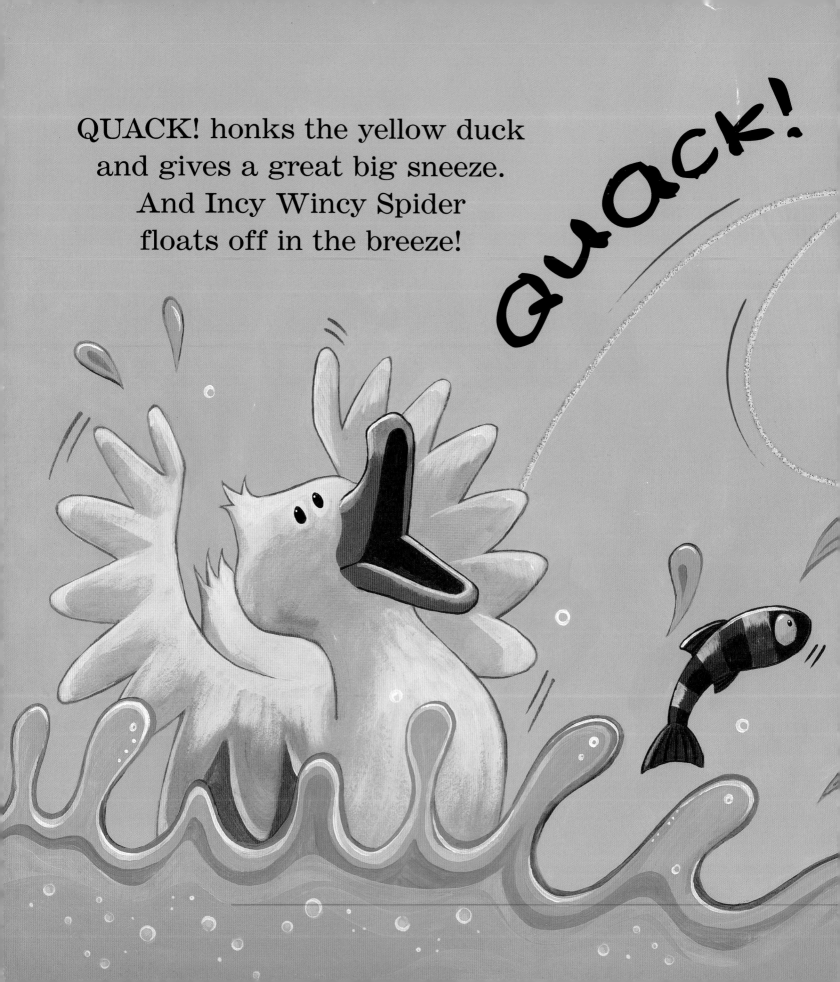

Incy Wincy Spider,
what a dizzy day!
He's settled on a brown horse
chewing clumps of hay.

Nei

NEIGHHHH! snorts the horse
and jumps up really high.
And Incy Wincy Spider
pings off through the sky!

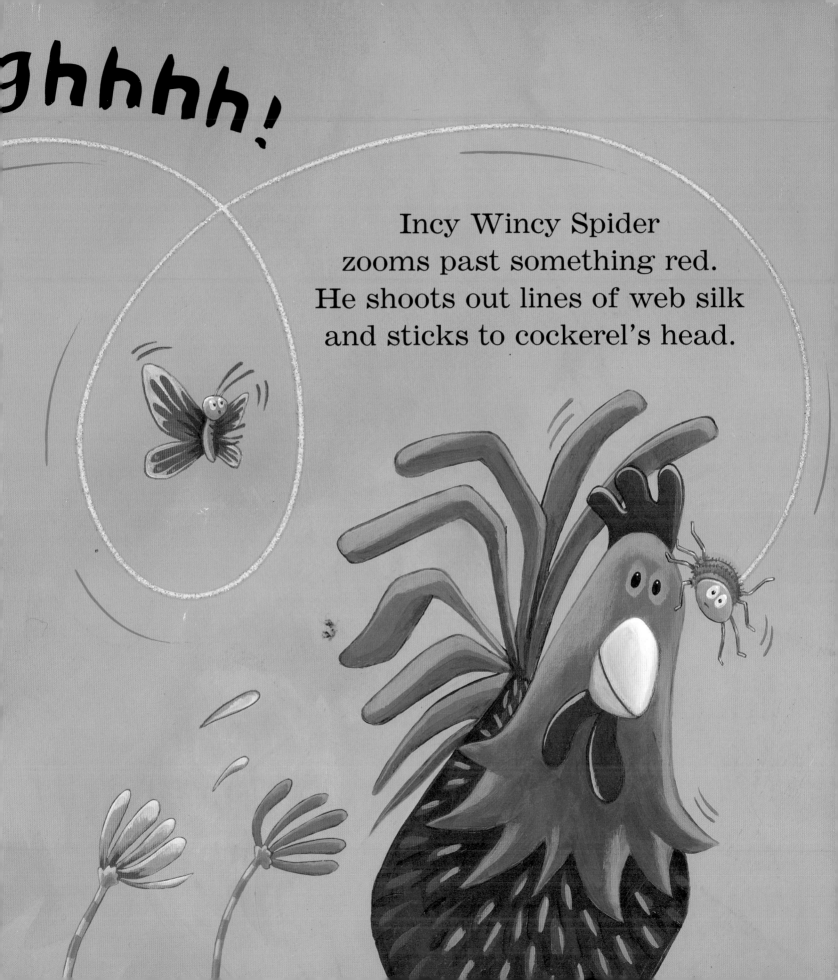

ghhhh!

Incy Wincy Spider
zooms past something red.
He shoots out lines of web silk
and sticks to cockerel's head.

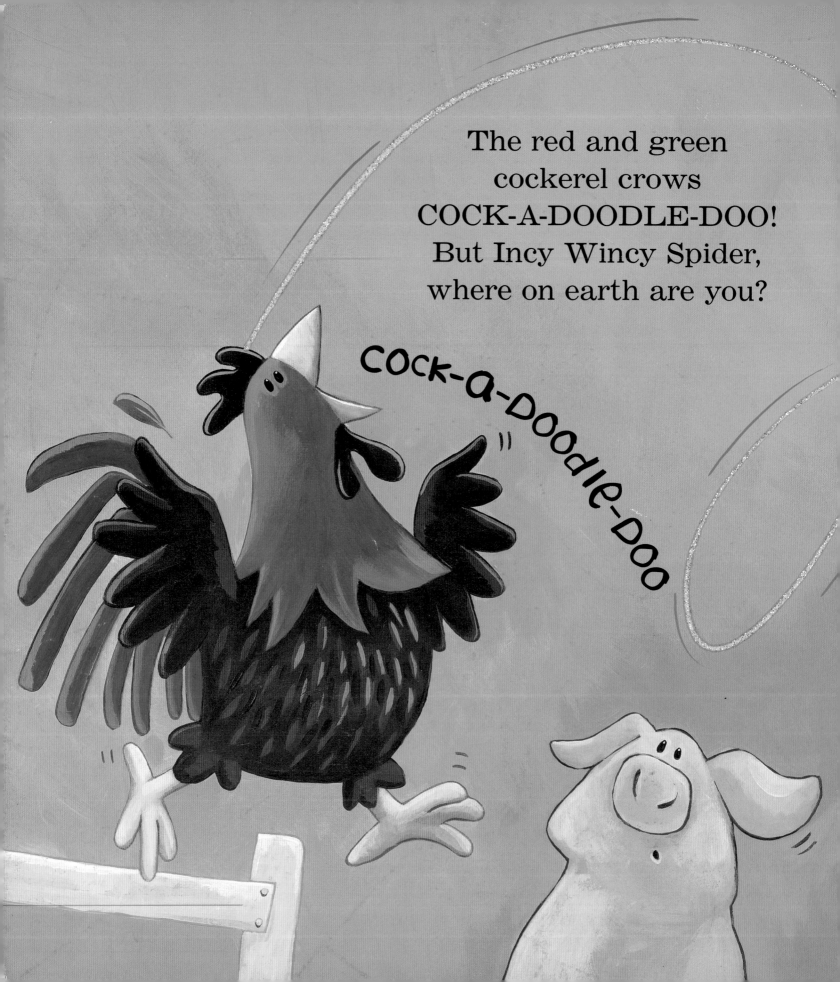

The red and green
cockerel crows
COCK-A-DOODLE-DOO!
But Incy Wincy Spider,
where on earth are you?

COCK-a-Doodle-DOO

Incy Wincy Spider,
what's he stuck on now?
A goat, horse or cockerel?
A pig, duck or cow?

No, he bounces with a

BOINNGGG!

Hooray! It's Mommy's web!
Now Incy Wincy Spider
is safely home in bed!

LITTLE TIGER PRESS
An imprint of Magi Publications
1 The Coda Centre, 189 Munster Road, London SW6 6AW
www.littletigerpress.com

First published in Great Britain 2005
This edition published 2010

Printed in China
LTP/1800/0059/0110

2 4 6 8 10 9 7 5 3 1